Dear Parents:

Children learn to read in stages, and all children develop reading skills at different ages. **Ready Readers**™ were created to promote children's interest in reading and to increase their reading skills. **Ready Readers**™ are written on two levels to accommodate children ranging in age from three through eight. These stages are meant to be used only as a guide.

Stage 1: Preschool-Grade 1
Stage 1 books are written in very short, simple sentences with large type. They are perfect for children who are getting ready to read or are just becoming familiar with reading on their own.

Stage 2: Grades 1-3
Stage 2 books have longer sentences and are a bit more complex. They are suitable for children who are able to read but still may need help.

All the **Ready Readers**™ tell varied, easy-to-follow stories and are colorfully illustrated. Reading will be fun, and soon your child will not only be ready, but eager to read.

GOLDIE'S NEW DOGHOUSE

Written by Agatha Brown
Illustrated by Vernon McKissack

Modern Publishing
A Division of Unisystems, Inc.
New York, New York 10022

Sandy Beaver loves his
new puppy, Goldie.

He wanted to build a doghouse for Goldie.

Tony Toucan is Sandy's friend.
"I want to help," Tony said.

Pat the Pony is also
Sandy's friend.
"I want to help," Pat said.

"And so do I," said
Ellie Elephant.

"Let's make a picture of what the doghouse should look like," Sandy said.

The four friends were very busy.

Everyone liked Sandy's drawing
the best.
"Now it is time to get the wood,"
Sandy said, "We need...

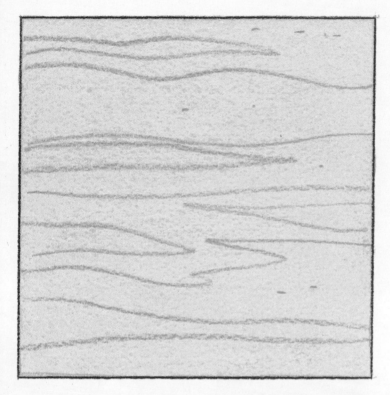

a square,

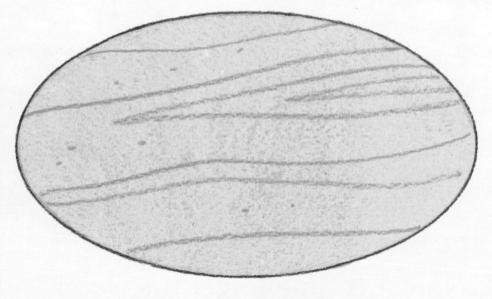

an oval,

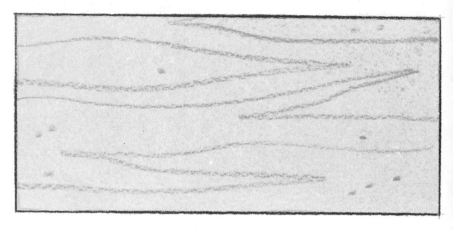

a rectangle,

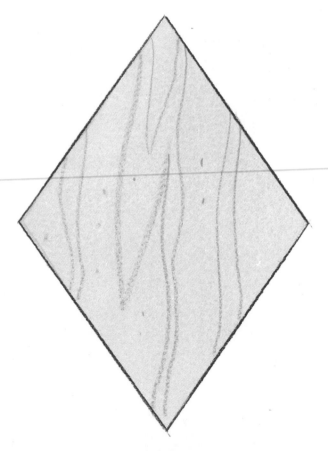

and a diamond.

We need a triangle, a crescent,

a circle and a star."

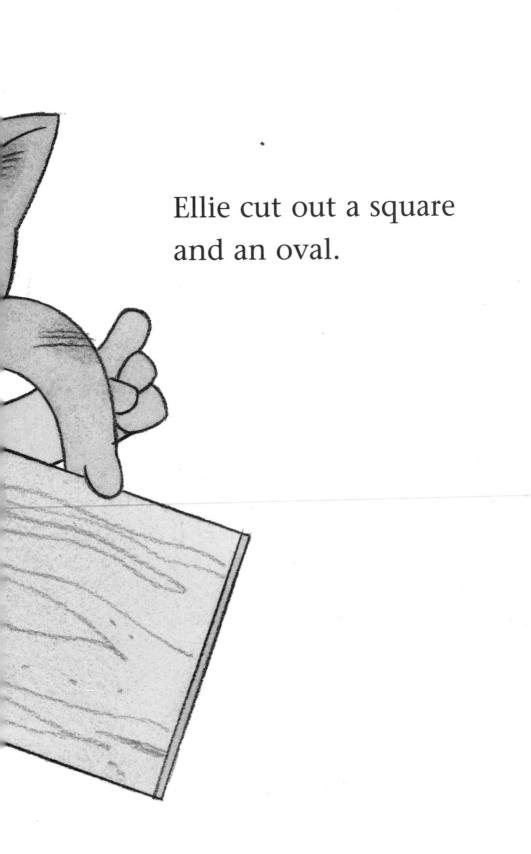

Ellie cut out a square
and an oval.

Pat cut out a diamond
and a rectangle.

Tony, Ellie, and Pat cut out all the other shapes. Then BANG! BANG! BANG! Sandy built the doghouse.

Soon he called his friends to see Goldie's doghouse.

"It looks good," Tony said.
"It looks great," Pat said.
"It looks grand," Ellie said.

And Goldie loved it very much!